A NOTE TO PARENTS

Reading Aloud with Your Child
Research shows that reading books aloud is the single most valuable support parents can provide in helping children learn to read.
- Be a ham! The more enthusiasm you display, the more your child will enjoy the book.
- Run your finger underneath the words as you read to signal that the print carries the story.
- Leave time for examining the illustrations more closely; encourage your child to find things in the pictures.
- Invite your youngster to join in whenever there's a repeated phrase in the text.
- Link up events in the book with similar events in your child's life.
- If your child asks a question, stop and answer it. The book can be a means to learning more about your child's thoughts.

Listening to Your Child Read Aloud
The support of your attention and praise is absolutely crucial to your child's continuing efforts to learn to read.
- If your child is learning to read and asks for a word, give it immediately so that the meaning of the story is not interrupted. DO NOT ask your child to sound out the word.
- On the other hand, if your child initiates the act of sounding out, don't intervene.
- If your child is reading along and makes what is called a miscue, listen for the sense of the miscue. If the word "road" is substituted for the word "street," for instance, no meaning is lost. Don't stop the reading for a correction.
- If the miscue makes no sense (for example, "horse" for "house"), ask your child to reread the sentence because you're not sure you understand what's just been read.
- Above all else, enjoy your child's growing command of print and make sure you give lots of praise. *You are your child's first teacher — and the most important one. Praise from you is critical for further risk-taking and learning.*

— Priscilla Lynch
Ph.D., New York University
Educational Consultant

D0360337

To S. V. Y.
—J. Y.

Copyright © 1995 by James Young.
All rights reserved. Published by Scholastic Inc.
HELLO READER!, CARTWHEEL BOOKS, and the CARTWHEEL BOOKS logo
are registered trademarks of Scholastic Inc.

Library of Congress Cataloging-in-Publication Data
Young, James, 1956-
   The cows are in the corn / by James Young.
      p.   cm. — (Hello reader! Level 2)
   Summary: Everyone in the family is upset when the farm animals get into the crops, but Mother remains calm and knows just what to do.
   ISBN 0-590-26601-2
   [1. Domestic animals—Fiction.   2. Farm life—Fiction.   3. Stories in rhyme.]   I. Title.   II. Series.
PZ8.3.Y787Co   1995   94-39099
[E]—dc20   CIP
                                                                  AC

23 22 21 20 19 18 17   0/0

Printed in the U.S.A.   23

First Scholastic printing, April 1995

The Cows Are in the Corn

by James Young

Hello Reader! — Level 2

SCHOLASTIC INC.

New York   Toronto   London   Auckland   Sydney

Brother woke up

and he began to shout,

"The cows are in the corn and they won't come out!"

Brother told Sister
and she began to shout,

"The pigs are in the figs
and they won't come out!"

Sister told Uncle
and he began to shout,

"The goats are in the oats
and they won't come out!"

Uncle told Auntie
and she began to shout,

"The rams are in the yams and they won't come out!"

Auntie told Father
and he began to shout,

"The bees are in the peas
and they won't come out!"

Father told Mother
and she didn't shout.
She didn't shudder
and she didn't pout.

She grabbed her big ladle
and she waved it all about.

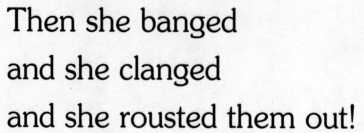

Then she banged
and she clanged
and she rousted them out!